Valentine's Gift

Femdom Hypnosis and Mind Control Micro-Fiction

S.B.

This e-book is dedicated to all hypnotic women and those that gladly follow their lead.

A special thank you to all patrons of Spell... B-O-U-N-D for the gift of their continued support.

Table of Contents

Introduction

The greatest gift you can give a woman is your obedience, submission, and everlasting loyalty. This is true every single day. However, why not go the extra mile on Valentine's day and let your kinky side come forth in all its splendor?

This new anthology allows you to do just that. Let your thoughts go blank in the presence of their mesmerizing power and discover bliss like no other. Have fun.

Class A Emergency

"Madam President, we have a problem."

"What's wrong, Dave?"

"Lab 7 has been compromised. A culture of Class A Nano-bots has been inadvertently released in the ventilation system and started to rewrite the DNA of everyone in the premises. We sealed off the building, but I'm afraid we'll need..."

"Say no more! Burn them all!"

Reborn

The silver sphere floated in the middle of the room, its radiance enveloping all members of the expedition.

"It actually exists!" Lisa said, bewildered, as she reached for the mystic object.

She was forever changed upon touching it, reborn as a goddess demanding absolute worship.

Now, she's on the move…

… coming for us all!

Valentine's Gift

"Will you be my Valentine Slave?"

That's all the card said, but it was enough to drive him crazy. Stephen read it time and time again, the words growing bigger, everything else shrinking....

Sitting in bed, his sister waited patiently for his submission. It shouldn't be long now, and she would definitely enjoy her gift.

Tibetan Relaxation

"How was your trip to Tibet, dear?"

"Oh, what can I say? Simply wonderful! A truly riveting experience!"

"Did the monks treat you well?"

"More than well, actually. Being around them was so... relaxing. I can still hear their chants in my head and... hmmm... I feel..."

"... ready to obey my will, slave?"

"Yes, Mistress."

Unholy Fruit

Though the apple looked grey and withered, it was actually quite succulent, just like the old gypsy woman had told her.

After the first bite, Andrew felt the tendrils of darkness spreading inside his mind and wiping it clean in a rush of ecstatic bliss he couldn't possibly resist.

Not that he tried to, anyway.

Miss Reaper

"Miss, I'm immune to every sales pitch in the universe so whatever it is you're selling, I'm not interested," he said, angrily.

The red-haired woman gave him half a smile.

"But this is a special vacuum cleaner... Its specialty is sucking souls."

At the press of a button, the life he knew ceased to exist.

Silence

We talked again, last night. At least, I think we did. I vaguely recall her infectious laugh, the rain in the background, and then... Silence. Not the kind you get in the absence of sound, but rather what lies beyond Music itself.

Deep down, I know I'm being played into surrender, and I don't care.

Happy New Year!

December 31st BM

Darren went to bed, her words floating in his mind. They spoke of a time to come, a new paradigm of self.

January 1st MT

Darren woke up, fully aware that the time was now and that nothing would ever change again. Towering proudly over him, she said:

"Happy New Year, slave!"

Poetic Memory

"Metaphors are dangerous. Love begins with a metaphor. Which is to say, love begins at the point when a woman enters her first word into our poetic memory," Benjamin muttered, dreamily.

"Theroux?" Sally asked.

"Kundera."

"That's how hypnosis begins too, but you love the danger, don't you?"

"I love you," he said, kissing her feet.

Serious Offense

"I didn't do a thing, officer!" the angry driver protested.

"I have evidence to the contrary. Leaving the scene of an accident is a serious offense. You know what happens to serious offenders, don't you?" the policewoman inquired.

"You take away my driver's license?"

"Yes, and much more than that..."

Her badge began to shine.

The Promise

"Ready?" Lacey asked.

"Yes," Drew responded, already lying down. "but promise me one thing. Promise you'll never lie to me because if you do, and I find out, it's all over."

"I promise. Do you promise to do the same?"

"I promise."

"Perfect," she smiled. The metronome started ticking as he allowed himself to relax.

Capitulation

"I will not submit," Uhr, the King of Careth, spat.

"You already did," Queen Vayla mocked. "Isn't your Seal all over the Declaration of Surrender?"

"I was drugged, bewitched!"

"And that shall continue 'til the day you die, slave-king. Hoist the colors!" She commanded.

Femmina's flag began to rise as his eyes sank into nothingness.

No Turning Back

Michael knelt, mesmerized by the twirling collar, a perfect symbol of power.

"You do realize that, if I do this, you'll lose your free will forever, right?" Theresa reminded him, pulling him even deeper.

"Y-yes," he stammered, not out of fear but overwhelming arousal.

The twirl became a spiral, and the spiral a blurry haze...

Appearances

All seems fine. No surprises. Life as usual.

Think again.

Something is different.

Time is moving backward, and you do not see it.

Words are cascading all around and you do not hear them.

You are captured, transfixed, empty with the fullness of her smile.

All seems fine. It is not.

It is absolutely perfect.

Nightmare Programming

"Hello, I'm Trent, hypnoslave..."

"Hi, Trent," a choir of voices was heard in reply.

"... and I'm running away from my Mistress," he continued.

The voices were outraged.

"What? How could you? Repent! Repent! REPENT!"

Trent woke up, drenched in sweat. Running away? What a nightmare!

"Never, Mistress," he muttered.

Standing by the door, she smirked.

Sometimes, Shit Happens… On Purpose!

"Yes, Mrs. Sanderson, we received the mp3s in question and reviewed them, accordingly, even going against company's policies. And no, we're still not paying for your husband's surgery, but all the associates are more than eager to try out your new toys, especially The Black Giant Monstrosity and The Swizzle Stick from Hell. Thank you!"

His Brightest Star

Dan stood by the tombstone, face down, adrift in one last dream.

All around, the world was broken into dull shards of frozen tears. Thoughts were suspended by the realization of the inevitable loss. The trance would fade away, but not the memories of beautiful night skies.

His brightest star was her. Rest in peace.

Levitation

Stanley and Gina's teaching habits couldn't be any more different. He would tolerate no levity in the classroom, while she encouraged levitation.

"What does that even mean?" he asked, one day, as he caught her by the water dispenser.

Choosing hot water, she made bubbles rise before his eyes.

He's been floating happily ever since.

Trips

"You're doing it again, Bianca."

"What?"

"The guilt trip, trying to make me mad, then pretend you're upset to control me further."

"You honestly think me capable of that, Cal?"

"Yes, but please don't."

"Another kind of trip then," she smirked, turning on the strobe light.

He would feel no guilt whatsoever in no time.

Her Dreams

The writer approached the Muse, carrying a club.

"I've come to claim Inspiration!" he shouted.

"Did you?" She yawned. "That's great, but..."

"But what?"

"You're dreaming, and you can't really control your dreams, mortal one."

She could though and, in her dreams, her feet were the paper, and his lips, the pen.

Time to write.

Rebuilt

The mirror was broken, just like him.

An eye here, an ear there, his lips by the corner, withered.

She came inside, soundlessly, swept the shards away and, with a finger snap, said: "Wake up."

He opened his eyes, looked into hers, and finally saw the collar around his neck. It was a perfect fit.

The Flying Consciousness

The waves were crashing, threatening to sink the world. She stood on the deck, spinning the wheel, as sparks from the thunderous skies above reflected on her eyes and then on his.

"This isn't real," he muttered, afraid.

"It will be..." she beckoned, pulling the sail from his heart.

Together, they made the ship fly.

Birthday Robot

"God, I'm so tired."

"Busy day?"

"Excruciating. Look, whatever plans you made for my birthday, please postpone them, okay?"

"You don't really want that, dear."

"Yes, I do, Jane, so please..."

"No, you don't. Activate ST3PH Protocol!"

Arms whirred, legs stiffened, and an oil change became in order... or should I just say, 'an order'?

The Right Thoughts

"Everything's broken."

"Are you sure?"

"That's what my thoughts are telling me."

"Thoughts are often wrong."

"Are there any right ones then?"

"I know a few."

Gently, she touched his face.

"What are you thinking now?"

"What you want me to think."

"Which is...?"

"You still my mind. I love you."

"I love you too."

Creativity

"Slow down a bit," Annabeth whispered.

"I can't right now," Luke responded, filling the canvas with violent strokes of ink.

"If you do, I can create something beautiful," she continued.

"Like what?"

"Sleep for me now."

He closed his eyes and her voice unearthed a new brush, painting every corner of his mind with love.

Liquid Dominance

"Are you sure it will work?" Steph asked, in fear.

"Absolutely," Dana replied. "My tonic will unleash your innermost desires."

Steph took a sip and felt the liquid dominance overwhelm her submissive nature.

"Yummy!" She exclaimed.

"I know. Now what?"

"Bend over, slave..."

"Yes?" Dana's eyes glimmered.

"... and make me a supply for a lifetime!"

Again and Again

"Come again?"

"Stop saying that, Di!" Mark shuddered.

"Come again?"

"Please stop!" he begged once more.

"Why? It's not my fault you're still susceptible to a post-hypnotic suggestion from a decade ago!"

"Come again? You planted that one, yesterday!"

"Made you say it..." she winked as the stain in his pants grew bigger and bigger.

Time to Suck

"So I couldn't beat your game, huh?" Harrison gloated. "Well, I just did, Pat... Suck it!"

"I'll leave that to you... Enjoy the credits!" She grinned.

He looked at the TV, now filled with kaleidoscopic reflections and images of strap-ons flashing in quick succession and froze.

He would suck big time from that day forward.

Mutation

"Another virus?!" Dr. Gregson said, dismayed.

"It's the same one, it mutated," Dr. Allen responded.

"So men are no longer behaving like chickens?"

"Now they think they're dogs."

"Have we been able to identify the source yet?"

"Experts are saying The Convention Center."

"Where that famous hypnotist is performing? You don't think she...?"

"Nah."

"Right..."

Gemini

"Get that pocket watch out of my face!"

"Hmmm, I love it, but why just one?"

"Stop it already, I don't want to go under!"

"So good... slipping, falling... please, I need to go deeper."

"Ah, I told you I would resist you, didn't I?"

"No power... no will left..."

SNAP

"Yes, Mistress."

"Yes, Mistress."

Loop

"Why are you calling me, Jen? It's 3 am."

"You're the one calling, Sam."

"Oh... why did I do that?"

"You tell me. Did you check your voicemail just now?"

"No."

"Are you sure?"

"Positive. Why?"

"It's nothing. Good night."

"Good night."

Intrigued, he checked his voicemail...

... and called her again, and again, and again...

Simulation

"Warning, mental shutdown imminent! Please press the 'abort' button," the computerized voice said.

Vernon complied and felt relieved when the Simulation Chamber's door opened.

"For a moment, I really thought I was going to succumb," he declared.

"But you didn't, right?" Trish asked.

"Of course not," he muttered as he crawled to kiss her ass.

Mentally Young

William Dawson was all the rage on the dance floor.

"Dad's looking lively!" Amber noted. "What happened?"

"You know that saying: 'you are only as old as you remember you are'?" her mother replied.

"Yes."

"Well, when he's hypnotized, he doesn't remember he's eighty-two anymore."

"How old does he think he is?"

"Sixty-nine," she winked.

The Ceremony

"Do you, Casey, take this woman to be your wedded wife and hypnotic Mistress, and promise to always obey her commands whether entranced or not?" The officiant asked.

"I do."

"And do you, Stella, take this..."

"Yes, I do," she snapped her fingers. "Sleep."

As the guests sank one by one, she raised her dress...

Sensibility and Mind Control

The water on the bowl was at 5 degrees Celsius.

"It's boiling!" Jack protested.

It was pitch black in the room.

"Turn off the lights! I'm going blind!" He begged.

A feather slid down his back.

"I'm being whipped!" He screamed.

As she fed him countless suggestions, Agnes was reminded why she loved sensation play.

Gridlock

"I have come to rescue you, my princess," Alan declared, head over heels.

"Finally! Oh, my knight in shining armor! What took you so long?" Bridget asked.

"There were giants, witches, and brightly-colored traffic lights and... wait, what?"

"Just relax and go deeper, dear," she cooed.

Who said being stuck in traffic couldn't be fun?

Fetish Love

He saw the leather boots and his heart started racing.

"You love these, don't you?" She hummed.

He did, of course. He loved everything she said he loved. He loved loving his ever-growing hypnotic obsession.

"Do you know what else you love?"

Gazing at the mirror, the answer was clear. Shame about the heels though.

Spree

"One thousand, three hundred and twenty-seven dollars, please," the shop clerk said.

"For a pair of shoes?!" Liam blinked.

"Sir?"

He blinked again, finally noticing the dozen bags on the counter, filled with dresses and sexy lingerie. Behind him, Dahlia toyed with his wallet.

Running into his Hypnodomme while shopping was always a dangerous proposition.

No Need

"Please... I need...!" Harrison implored.

"Need?" Portia scoffed. "No, you want to, and you shouldn't because you want what I want."

"I want what you want," he droned, dutifully conditioned.

"Dismissed."

"Yes, Mistress," he smiled sheepishly, a warm liquid sliding down his legs.

She was right. He didn't need to use the bathroom at all.

All Three

"Microsoft won E3!" Paul said.

"Excuse me?" Aaron rebuffed. "Sony won E3!"

"You guys are funny..." Dean laughed. "Nintendo won E3!"

Samantha rolled her eyes, snapped her fingers.

"I win all three," she declared, pulling them deeper and deeper under her spell.

The performances on the show floor were about to get way more interesting.

Mindless Accusation

"Why are you so angry?" Ashley asked.

"Because you hypnotized me with that ring!" Clive vociferated.

"Preposterous!" She raised her voice. "I did no such thing! Take back that mindless accusation... now!"

"S-sorry," he trembled.

"That's more like it. You're forgiven," she kissed him on the right cheek. "By the way... I used my lipstick."

Upgrade

The message on the screen read:

"An updated version of your mind is available. Click the button below to download."

Lester followed the instructions, smiling as the new strings of commands of his Mistress came to life. When it was over, the words "toenail muncher" flashed inside his brain.

Lunch was going to be scrumptious.

Healthy Hydration

"How's your diet, Jake?" His brother, Anthony, asked.

"Wonderful. Melissa has been helping me with her hypnotic skills. I already lost three pounds in two weeks!"

"Not bad."

"Jake?" Melissa intervened, dropping her skirt.

"Yes, dear?" He responded, eyes glazing.

"It's time for today's fluid intake."

"Yes, dear," he immediately knelt.

Who needs water anyway?

A Different Story

"And then she hypnotized him and lived happily after," Marjorie concluded.

"Your stories always end up the same way," Luke protested.

"That's not true. Take ours for instance."

"What about it?"

"I'm not going to do anything to you."

"Good."

"Can't say the same about your mother and sister though. Don't wait up for me."

Cheesy

"Cheese makes you forget," Joseph's mother always told him but he never listened. His favorite was Blue Stilton and a glass of Port. That would never change.

"Cheese makes you forget," Marguerite whispered, and he listened. He believed everything she told him like a good mindless puppet. That would never change.

Care for a slice?

Changing the Subject

"Stop changing the subject, Joan!" Clive begged.

"Why would I do that when the subject…," she paused "… likes to be changed?"

"That's not what I meant!"

"So you like it when I change your thoughts?"

"I didn't say that either!"

"Now who's changing the subject?"

"I… You… don't know."

She was counting on that.

Typing Slave

"T-ten thousand lines?" Derrick gasped.

"That's the price of disobedience," Cassandra declared.

"But I'll never be able to..."

"You'll type 'til you drop... slave!" She hissed.

"Yes, Mistress," he muttered as he began reproducing her commands.

He dropped into a trance after two hundred lines.

It would only take one before the week was done.

IKD

The calendar atop Marcia's desk had the following message scribbled in red lipstick: International Kissing Day. What better occasion to test her new mesmerizing lip gloss?

Leaving her office, she kissed three people. They felt compelled to kiss her in return.

Her boss kissed her feet.

His assistant kissed her ass.

His wife kissed her...

A Break

"Nadine?"

"What's wrong, Emil?"

"This thing between us... It can't be 24/7. I need a break."

"I know, which is why I'm giving you one minute of clarity."

"But that's not enou...!"

"Time's up. Sleep!"

His mind slammed shut.

"Hmmm... what was I doing?"

"You were about to kiss my shoes, Emily."

"Yes, Mistress."

Family Dinner

Deborah looked at her cousin John.

"You haven't touched your food."

He nodded in reply.

"Nor your drink."

He nodded again.

"Afraid to be drugged and turned into my obedient pet? "

"Yes."

"I'm smart enough not to pull the same stunt again..."

"Good."

"... so I tampered with your seat."

He wouldn't stay seated for long.

Six

"It's been six months..." Samantha smiled.

"Really? It only feels like six seconds," Brian retorted.

"Time flows differently in trance, dear."

"Huh? But you said you didn't want to do that to me."

"I don't remember that. Surprised you do though."

"Remember what?"

"Nothing. It's been six months..."

"Really? It only feels like six seconds."

In Print

"This is your idea of hypnosis?" Patrick grumbled.

"Keep looking, please," Elizabeth asked.

"Fine."

The printer continued running, bringing to life copies of a boring document. One by one, he saw them emerge, the colors of each new replica beginning to fade as the ink ran dry until everything went blank.

"Let's begin," she smirked.

Syndrome

"Are you still crying over Astrid?" John asked.

"Yes," Ben replied, eyes cast down.

"Why? She drugged you, brainwashed you, and practically ruined your life in the process!"

"I know but she was my Mistress. I miss her."

"Me too..." John finally admitted.

He sat next to his friend and sighed, thinking of Stockholm nights.

Inner Voice

"You need to write a story in fifty-five words."

"I know."

"It must have female dominance and mind control at its core."

"True."

"The four preceding lines had a total of twenty-three words."

"Really?"

"You've reached thirty-eight now."

"Okay."

"Only thirteen left."

"Huh?"

"Eleven."

"Sneaky countdown, huh?"

"Perhaps. Seven."

"Six?"

"Just finish already."

"Yes, Muse."

Missing Her

"I miss you..." Bradley admitted.

"You miss me or the way I made you feel?" Jenna asked.

"You. Every single day. Your voice. Your words..."

"You are conditioned. Would you still miss me even if I never hypnotized you again?"

"Yes. Yes. A thousand times Yes!"

"Good, but until then..."

Orgasmic bliss filled the room.

Conclusion

Well… how are you feeling right now? Are you ready to melt into a submissive puddle for the one that is sure to always control your mind and keep you safe? I hope so. Honor the gift of her dominance with the gift of your true soul and you are sure to find everything you need, and this is no fiction. For other creative escapades especially created to keep your juices flowing head over to my personal website - https://www.sbspellbound.net - and enjoy yourself as much as possible. Thank you.